Eugene E. Carlough
October 8, 1968

Meg

Do You Ever Feel Lonely?

by Rosalind Welcher
published by
Panda Prints, Inc.   New York

Do you ever feel Lonely?

Do you ever feel that NO ONE

really cares

that NO ONE UNDERSTANDS

that no one listens

that everyone is so busy

so involved

that Nothing you say

OR do

MAKES ANY IMPRESSION

that all you want is to be happy

IN YOUR OWN WAY

without any FUSS

OR bother

do you ever wonder who you
Really are

and what you REALLY want

do you ever feel lost...

bewildered

OUT OF TUNE

do you ever feel that nothing

really matters

and that you matter least of all

Do you ever feel lonely?

I did

UNTIL I met you

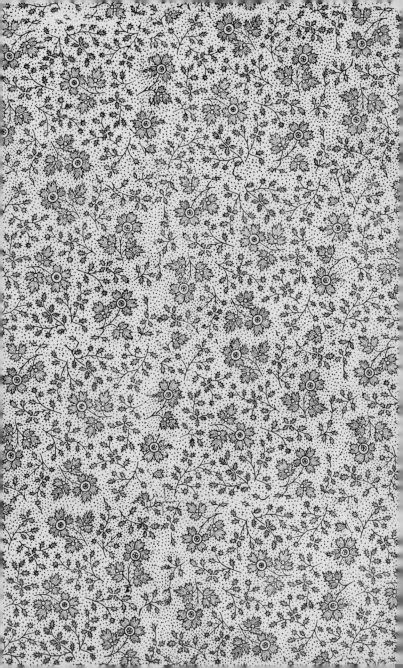